UNICORNS OF THE ISLE
Elle's Secret Wish

Elle was so pleased to be sharing her special day with the unicorns and pegacorns from the island. She was so grateful for their friendship. "I have the best unicorn friends in all of Avonlea," she said with a neigh. Despite all of this, Elle still felt a bit sad. For Elle secretly had one wish.

The Unicorn Tales series

UNICORN TALES
Elle's Secret Wish

AMIE BORST
illustrated by Roch Hercka

Summary: When a birthday wish leads to a surprise bigger
than Elle could have ever expected, she must brave the
unknown to find it.
BISAC: JUVENILE FICTION/Animals/Dragons,
Unicorns & Mythical. JUVENILE FICTION/Legends,
Myths & Fables/General. JUVENILE FICTION/Holidays
& Celebrations/Birthdays. JUVENILE
FICION/Concepts/Seasons.
For more information about this title, write us at Mystery
Goose Press P.O. Box 86627 Vint Hill, VA 20187

Printed in the United States of America.
Library of Congress Control Number: 2020910491
Paperback ISBN: 978-1-948882-15-6
Also available as an ebook.

ELLE'S SECRET WISH

AMIE BORST

Illustrated by
ROCH HERCKA

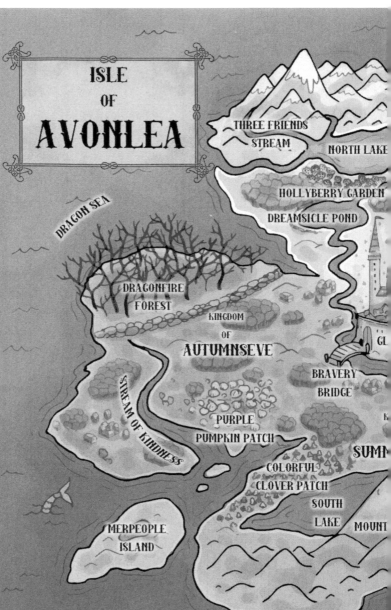

MOUNT WINTERSEND

INGDOM
OF
TERSEND

FAIRY
FOREST

CE

BLOSSOM
LAGOON

PIXIE PLACE

STAR HOLLOW

KINGDOM
OF
SPRINGSMORN

RAINBOW RIVER

SPARKLE FRUIT GARDEN

T

WILL-O'-THE-WISP
WOODS

ART

N
W   E
S

DRAGON SEA

Kingdom of Summerstart

Summerstart Kingdom has clouds of white.
Summerstart clovers grow day and night.
Adventure and magic and lots of heart,
This is the kingdom of Summerstart.

Chapter 1

*E*lle stood on the top of Mount Summerstart looking out over her kingdom. It was her birthday and she was excited for the special celebration that was soon to start.

As she waited for the guests to arrive, she marveled at the beauty of her kingdom. Summer was in full bloom. Trees were lush with green leaves, plants were bright with color, and blossoms of all variety dotted the landscape with fragrant beauty. Bees pollinated the Colorful Clover Patch. Butterflies, in a rainbow of colors, flittered about on the breeze.

Many times, Elle spent her days standing in front of the big picture window of her mansion overlooking her kingdom. She would watch as the unicorns of Summerstart pranced around the Colorful Clover Patch. Other times she saw them swimming in South Lake. There was one place in Summerstart, however, that the unicorns avoided. That place was Will-o'-the-Wisp Woods. It had several strange tales of spooks. Elle never wanted to go there.

The glory of Summerstart Kingdom brought Elle so much joy and she was grateful for her important job. Elle made sure the plants grew, especially the clovers that fed the unicorns all year long. As a peaceable unicorn, the others in the kingdom were happy to do as she asked. Together, they all helped maintain the clover crops and Elle was thankful for their service.

She watched now as a crowd gathered at the bottom of the mountain. Friends from the Kingdom of Summerstart—Bonnie, Maureen, and Anna—whinnied with excitement. Unicorns from the other kingdoms on the Isle of Avonlea joined the three friends and pranced about, neighing loudly.

Callie and Maribel flew side by side. They looped about in the sky, creating breezes that blew Elle's glittering golden mane. A trail of white from Callie's hooves melted almost instantly, turning into droplets of rain as she soared toward the mountain's peak. Maribel's wings made a powerful wind. It blew the rain into a misty shower which watered the blossoms and clovers below.

"Whoa," Elle said with a laugh as she watched the pegacorns in action. "Take it easy!"

Callie and Maribel slowed their flight until they landed gracefully on top of Mount Summerstart. Maribel carried a basket in her mouth which she placed on the ground. The two friends cantered toward Elle who reared up with excitement to greet them.

"Happy birthday, Elle!" the pegacorns sang in unison.

Elle smiled. "Thank you. I'm so glad you've come to my celebration!"

"We'd never miss it," Callie said as she shook her mane. A gift, wrapped in lavender colored paper, tumbled to the ground. A yellow ribbon with a perfectly shaped bow sparkled in the sunlight. "I chose gold to match your hair. And purple because it's your favorite color."

"That was so thoughtful of you, Callie." Elle picked up the gift, trotted into her mansion, and placed it on a decorated table. There were tiny purple stars scattered on the tabletop. Baskets of colorful clover, harvested by Maureen and

Anna, were proudly displayed. Green sparkle fruit glistened in a large bowl. Maeve, a unicorn from the Kingdom of Springsmorn, had been kind enough to deliver the fruit earlier that morning. "I'll open it later once the others arrive."

"I've brought you a gift, too. It isn't wrapped but here it is." Maribel placed a basket of pink hollyberries on the table.

"These are splendid!" Elle said as she popped a berry in her mouth. "They'll be perfect for sharing at the party. Thank you for being so thoughtful."

Maribel smiled. "I'm glad you like them. They're my favorite."

"As much as I love the clovers, I look forward to these hollyberries every year." Elle brushed shoulders with Maribel, thanking her for the present.

Elle then trotted toward a large window which overlooked her kingdom. The glass stretched from floor to ceiling. It also went from one wall to another. It was just as wide as it was tall. Crystals and pearls framed the window. The unicorns of Avonlea began to climb Mount Summerstart and Elle squealed with excitement. "Here they come!"

Elle's birthday had come to be known as the greatest celebration in all of Avonlea. Unicorns and pegacorns, from all the kingdoms on the entire Isle of Avonlea attended the party each year. As they marched, the unicorns hummed the tune of Summerstart Kingdom.

The unicorns each brought a gift with them. Some gifts, like the hollyberries from Maribel, were unique to their kingdoms. Other gifts were treasures that the unicorns had crafted using their magic. Though Elle always appreciated their thoughtfulness, she was more pleased they'd come to spend time with her.

There was a single truth that Elle knew and cherished. Gifts were a momentary thing. Friendships were forever.

One by one, the friends reached the top of the mountain. They each greeted Elle with a hello and their special gift. In return, Elle welcomed them into her glittering purple mansion.

Elle was so pleased to be sharing her special day with the unicorns and pegacorns from the island. She was so grateful for their friendship. "I have the best unicorn friends in all of Avonlea," she said with a neigh.

Despite all of this, Elle still felt a bit sad. For Elle secretly had one wish. A wish that she could never tell anyone.

Chapter 2

*E*lle wished to see a snowstorm. Just once, she wanted to go to the Kingdom of Wintersend. She hoped to see the wonderful white fall from the sky. She longed to frolic in the magic of winter. She wanted to attend the Snowflake Festival, see a frozen pond, build a snowman, and pick the pink hollyberries. Her friends from Wintersend told her the many stories of all the whimsical things in their kingdom. All of it sounded wonderful but she longed to see a snowstorm most of all. Elle wanted to see it for herself.

It was impossible, however, as Elle couldn't leave her post on top of Mount Summerstart. She was destined to stay in her mansion all the days of her life, never able to leave it or the Kingdom of Summerstart. In a way, Elle was a prisoner to the very kingdom she loved so very much. She knew her wish was an impossible one.

Elle was delighted to see her many friends, including Callie and Maribel. Their fur coats were cooler than any unicorn she'd ever known. She thought maybe that was what a snowstorm would feel like. She also wondered what a snowstorm looked like. Were snowflakes large or small? She'd once been told that each snowflake was different. Could that really be true? Elle had so many unanswered questions. Sure, many of them she could learn from her friends, but it wasn't quite the same as seeing it for herself. She refused to be unhappy about it even though it seemed to make her heart ache just a bit too much.

Elle shook her head and told herself to smile. She had so much. Never seeing a snow-storm wasn't so bad, even if her heart did long for this extra special birthday wish.

Soon more unicorns trotted into the mansion, each bringing a very special gift just for Elle. There were unicorns from all four kingdoms.

Callie, Maribel, Paisley, and Heidi – the

pegacorns – had flown from the Kingdom of Wintersend.

Maeve, Fiona, Jillian, and Shannon had made the long trek along the Rainbow River from their Kingdom of Springsmorn.

Elle's friends from the Kingdom of Summerstart—Bonnie, Maureen, and Anna—had all helped her get ready for the party.

Also joining the celebration were Nadia, Morgan, Keena, and Bridgette, the unicorns from the Kingdom of Autumnseve.

It was always the greatest honor when the twins, Genevieve and Guinevere, joined the party. Today, however, they had work to do at the Crystal Palace.

"Happy birthday, Elle!" the unicorns said as they entered through the mansion's door. "We hope you're excited for your special day."

"Hello, friends!" Elle said with a smile. "Thank you for coming to my birthday celebration."

"We wouldn't miss it for the world," Maureen said. "It's my favorite event of the summer."

"Well, it's always summer here," Bonnie said.

Maureen laughed. "That's true. I should say it's my favorite event in August."

Elle nodded. "It's mine, too." She laughed and so did the other unicorns.

"Now, where should we put these?" Bonnie nudged the wrapped gift perched on her shoulder. Maureen held up a gift bag with her teeth. The bag had a rainbow on it. The white clouds at the bottom of the rainbow sparkled with glitter the color of opals. Anna held a tiny box with a clover on it.

"I'll take them," Callie said. "I'll just put the gifts on the table over there." She nodded toward the decorated table, then clip-clopped off with the gifts for Elle.

When everyone was settled, they gathered together for the best part of the party. The unicorns were going to play games!

Chapter 3

"*P*in the tail on the mermaid is my favorite," Nadia, from the Kingdom of Autumseve, said. She could make rainbows appear anywhere she wanted. Nadia shook her bright pink mane. It was as vibrant and as beautiful as the very rainbows she created. It seemed everything she touched was colorful and bright. "We should play it first."

Fiona, from the Kingdom of Springsmorn, neighed. Everything she said sounded like music, as that was her magic. "It's Elle's birthday celebration. We should let her decide."

"What game would you like to play, Elle?" Maeve asked. She swished her tail and droplets of water splashed about.

"Hey, stop that," Morgan said. "You're getting me all wet." Morgan didn't like being splashed. It made her sparkling, firey horn fizzle out.

"Sorry," Maeve said. She closed her eyes and concentrated on controlling water.

"The fountain stopped running," Maribel cried, her tongue hanging from her mouth in mid-slurp. "Maeve? Did you do that?"

Maeve opened her eyes and saw the fountain was all dried up. "Oops! My mistake." She focused again and the water trickled into the fountain until it was bubbling like a brook.

"Much better," Maribel said as she took a drink. "It's very warm in the Kingdom of Summerstart. Much different than the cold, snowy climate of Wintersend. I felt like I might melt without a cool drink. That fountain is refreshing!" She giggled as water dripped from her mouth.

Maeve laughed. "Now, what were we doing?" she asked as she looked around the room. "Ah, yes! The game. Which one would you like to play, Elle?"

"Please say 'pin the tail on the mermaid,'" Nadia said. "It's my favorite." She then chanted the name of the game as Elle stared out the window. "Pin the tail on the mermaid, pin the tail on the mermaid, pin the tail on the mermaid, pin—"

"Stop saying that," Maeve said, flicking her tail at Nadia. A few droplets of water splashed into Nadia's face who frowned. Maeve turned her attention back to Elle. "What did you decide?"

"Huh?" Elle blinked. She tilted her head as she gazed at her friend. There was a far-away look in her eyes. "What was that?"

"The game." Bonnie squinted at Elle who was behaving oddly. "Maeve and Nadia would like to know which one you would like to play?"

"Oh, ummm..." Elle tried to think but she was distracted about her secret wish.

Nadia pointed at the mermaid game and smiled big.

Elle noticed where Nadia pointed. "Pin the tail on the mermaid sounds perfect."

Nadia jumped with excitement. "Yessss!" Then she used her magic to tack the gameboard to the wall. Each guest received a mermaid tail. Nadia looked at hers in disappointment. "I'm number sixteen," she said with a moan. "That means I'm last."

"Trade with me," Elle said passing her

mermaid tail to her guest. "I'm number one. You can go first."

"But I can't take that," Nadia said. "You're the birthday unicorn."

"That's right. I am the birthday unicorn and I say you get to be first." Elle nudged her friend, encouraging her to go to the head of the line.

"Are you sure?" Nadia whinnied softly.

Elle nodded. "Absolutely."

"Thanks, Elle," Nadia said. "It's no wonder your party is the best celebration of them all."

Elle bowed her head. She could be a gracious host, that was true, but it didn't change the longing in her heart to see a snowstorm. No amount of kindness would ever grant that kind of wish.

"Don't forget the blindfold!" Callie said. She trotted over to Nadia, carrying a sparkly purple mask. It had a white lace trim that Elle always imagined looked like snowflakes. Callie placed it over Nadia's eyes. "Now we need to spin you three times."

"I never liked this part!" Nadia said with a neigh. "I always get dizzy."

"You can do it! Now, let's see." Elle nudged Nadia's shoulder. The other unicorns trotted over, standing in a circle around Nadia. They spun her around and around. When they finished, Elle said, "Now it's time to pin that tail!"

Nadia stumbled from one side to the other, heading in the wrong direction. Elle could see Nadia was too dizzy to find her way. Elle had to think fast! She quickly took the game from the wall and followed by Nadia's side. The dizzy unicorn wobbled to and fro. As soon as Nadia approached a wall and started fumbling for the gameboard, Elle quickly pinned it up without Nadia knowing. Nadia placed her mermaid tail on the mermaid perfectly, thanks to Elle's help.

Callie smiled at Elle as she removed the blindfold from Nadia. All the other unicorns and pegacorns in the room giggled knowing what Elle had done to help Nadia win the game.

Nadia opened her eyes. "I did it!" she cried. "It's perfect, too!"

"You did a marvelous job," Elle said with a smile.

Callie chuckled. But as soon as Nadia turned around and looked at her, Callie bowed her head. She was good at keeping secrets. Elle was sure Callie would keep this one, too. She wouldn't reveal that Elle had helped Nadia with the game.

"Try to beat that!" Nadia said.

"I don't think we can," Callie said, still trying to conceal her laughter.

Elle blinked. "Anyone else want to try?"

The other unicorns lined up. Maeve went second, followed by Callie, Maribel, Fiona, Bonnie, and Morgan. The remaining unicorns, Paisley, Heidi, Jillian, Shannon, Maureen, Anna, Keena, and Brigette all took their turns. Elle went last. No one could do quite as well as Nadia.

"I won!" Nadia said. "I knew there was a reason this was my favorite game!"

Elle and Callie exchanged knowing glances. The other unicorns whinnied with laughter. Elle wouldn't reveal the secret and she was sure none of the other unicorns would either.

But Elle felt sad that it wasn't the only secret she was keeping. If only she could tell her friends about her wish to see a snowstorm.

Chapter 4

*A*fter the unicorns played games, Nadia and Morgan wheeled a cart into the center of the room. On top of the cart was a beautiful four-tiered birthday cake.

The bottom layer was the largest and had white frosting. A drawing of a pastel rainbow added beautiful color. Yellow daisies rimmed the cake like clouds.

Lavender colored roses trimmed the third layer which was frosted a soft shade of yellow.

The third layer was white, just like the bottom, and it had more yellow daisies

The fourth and final layer was also yellow. It was the most splendid of all. It was decorated to look just like Elle. The top of the cake had pretty eyes, a smile, and flowing golden hair. A yellow candle, meant to look like Elle's horn, flickered as it cast a glow into the room.

"I've never seen anything so beautiful!" Elle cried in delight. "What a marvelous cake!"

"Morgan made it herself," Nadia said.

Morgan blushed.

"You've out done yourself, Morgan," Elle said. "It's not just cake, it's art!"

"Well," Morgan said. "There's an extra special surprise just for you."

"Another surprise?" Elle's eyes grew wide. She'd never expected such a wonderful birthday celebration. This truly was the most spectacular one she'd ever had.

"Yes, but you'll just have to wait and see." Morgan lifted her chin in the air with a whinny.

Elle raised her eyebrow. "Hmmm...sounds interesting." She backed up and admired the cake from a distance.

"Dim the lights!" Callie called to Maribel who was across the room by the door. She flicked the light switch and the room went dark.

"Now, let's sing the birthday song!" Maeve said, trotting over closer to the cake. She bowed and sang a note that was off pitch. She didn't seem to notice her note was sour and smiled as she began to sing another note.

"Why don't you let me lead the music?"

Fiona forced her way through the crowd until she reached Maeve.

"But you lead every year," Maeve said. "I'm perfectly fine to sing. I'd like to lead just this once."

Fiona tipped her head. She knew Maeve was right. Plus, she couldn't tell her friend that her notes were off-pitch. That would be rude. She looked around the room at the unicorns of Avonlea who were staring wide-eyed at them. "Then you should lead," Fiona said. "You'll do a fine job." If the other unicorns didn't notice the sour notes, then Fiona would ignore it. It was Elle's birthday party after all. No sense in squabbling over silly things.

"Very well then," Maeve said. She opened her mouth, showing all of her teeth. She tipped her head back, ready to belt a loud note. Her horn hit a cluster of colorful balloons. There was a loud pop!

"Ahh!" a few unicorns screamed. Others startled and began to run in circles around the room.

"Everyone please remain calm," Elle said.

"But that noise could have been anything.

Maybe even something scary," Bonnie said as she looked around the mansion.

Callie neighed. "It could have even been a snow bear!"

"Don't be silly," Maribel said. "They wouldn't come to Summerstart. It's much too warm here."

"I see the problem," Fiona said. She trotted over to Elle with the remains of a balloon in her mouth. "Maeve must have popped it with her horn."

Maeve chuckled. "That's what it was!"

"Shall we get on with the party?" Bonnie asked. "It will be dark soon and…"

"You're afraid of the dark?" Morgan asked.

"I didn't say that!" Bonnie neighed loudly in defense. "But it is getting late. We shouldn't stay too long. It's Elle's special day. She should enjoy the rest of her birthday how she pleases."

"Alright then," Maeve said. "The birthday song it is." Maeve opened her mouth wide and tipped her head back again, making sure no more balloons were in the way. She began to sing the birthday song.

"Birthdays are for you…"

The rest of the unicorns joined in.

"Birthdays are for me..."

They all sang loudly and clear.

"Sparkles pink and blue..."

The unicorns sang even louder for the last line.

"In the land of Avonlea!"

When the unicorns finished singing, they all stomped their hooves on the floor. Some threw their heads back and neighed. Others, like Heidi, laughed with joy.

Elle glanced around the room at her friends. Many had traveled far just for her birthday celebration. She was so happy. Nothing brought her greater joy than her beautiful kingdom and her friendships. She truly had the best friends any unicorn could ever hope for.

Her throat suddenly got tight. She had everything a unicorn could ever want. Presents, a beautiful mansion, a peaceful kingdom, delicious food, and most important, good friends. The only thing she didn't have was her one dream to see a snowstorm. She'd longed for that wish to come true. But it felt so very selfish.

"It's time to blow out your candle," Maribel said.

"Go on, Elle!" Callie nudged. "What are you waiting for?"

Elle blinked. Her friends stood in silence staring back at her.

"Don't forget to make a wish." Morgan's firey horn sparkled.

The candle on the birthday cake flickered and sparked.

"A wish?" Elle's eyes grew wide as she looked at Morgan. Didn't Morgan also mention an extra special surprise?

"Yes, a wish. You just never know when it might be granted." Morgan smiled with a wink.

That's it! Elle thought. *That's what birthday candles are for!*

Elle pinched her eyes closed tight.

She pursed her lips.

I wish to see a snowstorm, she thought.

Then she blew out her candle.

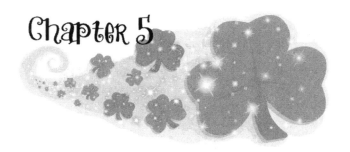

Chapter 5

*E*lle opened her eyes. The flame on her candle had gone out. A little puff of smoke in the shape of a star rose up into the air. She didn't feel any different though. That was the strange thing about birthdays. Even though you're a whole year older, it still feels the same.

She glanced around the room, looking at each of her friends. Maybe they felt a change. When she caught their gaze, she realized they were just the same as they were before, too.

Elle looked up at the ceiling of her mansion. Maybe the snowstorm was there waiting for her to notice it. But when she saw the ceiling covered in diamonds and pearls, the same as it was before, she knew her wish hadn't come true. There simply wasn't a snowstorm. There probably never would be. Such a wish was impossible.

"Let's eat!" Morgan said as she served each unicorn a slice of cake. She reserved the horn for Elle. "Hold onto this," she said as she gave it to the birthday unicorn. "You'll want it later."

The candle sparkled and glittered, tickling her hoof. "How very odd," Elle said.

"Birthday magic," Morgan whispered.

By the time the unicorns finished eating their cake, the sky had changed to a vibrant shade of orange.

"Sunset," Nadia said. "It's getting late."

"We better get back to our kingdoms or we'll have no choice but to stay the night." Callie reared up on her hind legs and spread out her wings. The unicorns ducked out of the way, neighing in agreement.

"Happy birthday, Elle," Maeve said. "I hope all your wishes come true."

Elle's eyes grew wide. She only had *one* wish. She couldn't stop thinking about it as she stared down at the glittering candle. Morgan had said some strange things. *Birthday magic...extra special...*was Morgan trying to trick her?

"Thank you," Elle said. "My wishes have already come true." She dipped her head knowing that wasn't the full truth. But she couldn't tell her guests what she really hoped for. If Callie knew Elle's secret wish, she was sure that Callie would do everything she could to make it come true.

It would be dangerous to bring a snowstorm to the Kingdom of Summerstart. And Elle could never leave her kingdom to see the snow in Wintersend. There was no other way to see a snowstorm. Elle would have to keep her wish a secret forever.

Callie rubbed her muzzle against Elle's as she said goodbye. "I'll see you next year!"

"Yes," Elle said. "Of course. I'll see you then." Saying goodbye was the part she disliked most about her birthday celebration. She wouldn't see many of her friends again for an entire year. That was such a pitiful long time to wait.

Maribel trotted up and brushed shoulders with Callie. The two left the party together.

Then Maeve and Fiona each walked up alongside Elle, rubbing their muzzle against hers. "Happy birthday," they said in unison.

"Thank you for a lovely party," Maeve said.

"I'm so grateful you could join me and bring such delicious sparkle fruit," Elle said.

Maeve bowed, shook her mane—showering

droplets of water everywhere—and then trotted out the door.

Elle stood watch as her friends made the long trek down Mount Summerstart. It would be a lonely year without her friends. Good thing she had plenty to keep her busy. She'd tend to her kingdom and make sure the colorful clovers were vibrant and plentiful.

After all of her friends were at the bottom of the hill, and were no bigger than a speck, Elle closed the door to her mansion. The remains of the birthday celebration were everywhere. Balloons floated about, streamers hung from the chandelier, and the candle from the top of her birthday cake still glittered like stars. She smiled at how thoughtful it was for Morgan to create such a beautiful work of art. She also still wondered about what Morgan had said.

Elle noticed all of the gifts on the table. She wouldn't open them now. She'd save them. When she was a much younger unicorn, she'd tear them open right in front of her guests, unable to contain her excitement. Now that she was older, she enjoyed saving them for days when she was lonely. It brought her so much joy to think of how clever and thoughtful her friends were.

One gift caught her eye as it sparkled and glistened. She hadn't noticed it before. Elle was sure she would have remembered. She crept toward it, unable to ignore the curiosity growing within her.

As Elle approached, she gasped. She was wrong. The sparkle wasn't from a gift. It was a reflection!

"Well, hello!" a voice called.

Elle swirled around.

A fairy stood in the middle of her living room!

Chapter 6

"Who are you?" Elle whinnied with surprise. She'd never seen a real-live fairy before.

"I'm Fairy Princess Gardengrow," the fairy said turning in a circle as her long dress covered in flowers swirled around her. She had golden hair and big green eyes that sparkled when she laughed.

"Nice to meet you," Elle said, watching the fairy in awe.

Gardengrow tapped a wand in her hand. The wand was bent in the middle and looked like a twig from a tree. Tiny colorful flowers bloomed from a green vine that wrapped around the stick. "I've come to grant your wish."

"My wish?" Elle stepped backward. *How could she know about my wish?*

"Yes. The one you made for your birthday."
Fairy Princess Gardengrow giggled. Her large,
butterfly-like wings fluttered, lifting her slightly
off the ground.

"But, I…" Elle's coat of gold shimmered as
she shook her mane in disbelief. She couldn't
believe what was happening. "I don't
understand."

"The candle." Fairy Princess Gardengrow
pointed her wand at the remains of Elle's
birthday cake where the candle now lay beside
it. "It was magic."

"A magic candle? Impossible!" There was no such thing as a magic candle. That's what fairy tales were made of. In fact, fairies weren't real, and neither were the tales that had been told about them. The only magic on the Isle of Avonlea were the unicorns. They could control the weather, the seasons, the water, the wind, the plants, and all manner of glorious things. "Don't be silly. There's no such thing."

"Oh, my! But it's true, my smart unicorn!" Fairy Princess Gardengrow fluttered into the air and tapped her wand on Elle's head. "There's magic all around us." The fairy twirled about in the air, circling the room. " Including all of the unicorns. And including this very special candle."

Elle wondered. *Did Morgan know the candle was magical? Is that why she reminded her to make a wish?* "Did Morgan ask you to do this?"

"You're a smart one." Fairy Princess Gardengrow flittered back down to the ground with a giggle. She paced in front of the window, her wings opening and closing with each step she took. "Now, what was it you wished for?"

My wish was to see a snowstorm, Elle thought.

She closed her eyes tight. *I wish to see a snow-storm!* Elle quickly opened her eyes.

Fairy Princess Gardengrow came to a sudden halt. "A-ha!" She pointed her wand to the ceiling. "I've got it! You wish to see a slugworm!"

Elle shook her head. "No, no thank you. I've seen plenty of them and they ruin the crops in the Colorful Clover Patch."

"That's not it? Hmmm….I'll just have to keep thinking then." Fairy Princess Gardengrow began to pace once again. "Oh, I know!" She stopped, pointed her wand at Elle, and said, "You wish to *be* a slugworm!"

"Ewwwhh!" Elle pinched her eyes closed and shook her head. "I would never want to be something that could harm the crops in Avonlea."

"Of course," Fairy Princess Gardengrow said with a chuckle. "How silly of me."

As Fairy Princess Gardengrow puzzled it out, Elle had a terrible thought. If Fairy Princess Gardengrow granted her wish it could spell disaster. *I can't let her guess my wish. If she does, it could ruin the kingdom. It may ruin all of Avonlea! How could I have been so selfish?*

Elle whinnied loudly. *Could she unwish a wish?* That's what she'd do! She blew on the candle, even though it didn't have a flame. She wished to herself, *I do **not** wish to see a snowstorm.*

"I have it this time!" Fairy Princess Gardengrow squealed.

Elle gasped. "You do?"

"Yes. You wish to be a glow swarm!"

Elle looked at the fairy in confusion. A glow swarm was a group of glowworms that flew together at night. She shook her head. "No, I didn't wish for that."

Fairy Princess Gardengrow squinted. "A crow dorm?"

"I don't even know what that is." Elle yawned, feeling tired.

"A show warm?"

Elle shook her head.

"A toe form?"

Elle looked at the fairy in confusion. "What are toes?"

"Know storm…" Fairy Princess Gardengrow tapped her chin as if she were trying really hard to recall Elle's wish.

"It's okay. I didn't wish for anything." Elle flicked her tail. It was best if Fairy Princess

Gardengrow didn't guess the wish. Then Avonlea would be safe. Elle would never wish for anything so dangerous ever again.

Fairy Princess Gardengrow looked right past Elle as she continued to make guesses about the wish.

"Really, it's fine." Elle looked out over the fairy's shoulder. The sun had set, and the sky had grown dark. She didn't realize they had been at this game for so long. Elle was beginning to feel very tired. It had been a big day. She wanted to sleep and wake just in time for morning tea. A big bowl of steamed hollyberry leaves sounded wonderful. "I promise you I didn't wish for anything," she said with a yawn.

Fairy Princess Gardengrow froze. "Are you certain?"

Elle nodded.

"Well, in that case then, I suppose I'll be on my way." The fairy turned toward the door.

Elle's heart leapt into her throat. She'd had a chance to see a snowstorm with this magical wish and she just gave it up! It was the right thing to do, though, because her wish would endanger all the unicorns on the Isle of Avonlea. It was better this way. She would dream of snowstorms instead. Once a year, she'd feel the coolness of the storm on Callie's coat. That would be enough. It had to be.

Fairy Princess Gardengrow turned her back to Elle and gazed out the window. "Very well then. If that's what you truly want." She sighed heavily.

Elle lowered her head. "It is."

"It's a pity, too," the fairy said with her hand on the doorknob. "Because I was just about to grant your wish to see a *snowstorm*."

*E*lle gasped so hard she choked. After a brief coughing fit, she stumbled forward, tripping over the table of gifts. "A snowstorm? Heavens no! I'd never wish for such a thing."

"Are you certain?" Fairy Princess Gardengrow furrowed her brow. Her lips drew in tight and formed a tiny bow.

"Yes," Elle nodded with a neigh. "A snowstorm would endanger my kingdom and the entire Island of Avonlea."

"Wishes are engraved in gold," Fairy Princess Gardengrow said, holding up a gold coin shaped like a clover. "And this one is yours." She held it out in her palm for Elle to see.

Sure enough, the coin had Elle's face on one side. On the other was her wish.

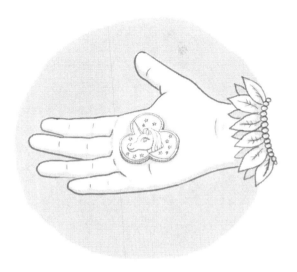

"Wishes can't be changed. And they cannot be denied."

Elle's chest ached. She began to breathe heavily. She thought she might faint. What had she done? This was terrible, awful, and it was all her fault. She should have never made that wish. She'd have to talk to Morgan about this. Elle looked at the ground. No, that wouldn't help anything. The only person she had to blame was herself. She should have wished for a bowl of sparkle fruit instead.

"Are you sure?" Elle shivered at the thought of the terrible thing she had done.

"I'm positive." Fairy Princess Gardengrow folded her arms with a nod. "All wishes must be granted."

Elle reared up, kicking her front hooves in the air. She landed with a clip-clop. "But what if I've changed my mind?"

"There's no going back, my smart unicorn." Fairy Princess Gardengrow flitted toward Elle and patted her softly. "Now don't you worry. This won't hurt a bit." Then Fairy Princess Gardengrow lifted her wand high into the air and swirled it about overhead. A trail of fairy dust flurried in the air, swirling about like a tornado. The fairy quickly brought her wand down. As she was about to tap Elle on her sparkly gold horn, the unicorn backed away.

"Wait a minute!" Elle cried. "I can't. I can't have you grant my wish."

Fairy Princess Gardengrow's wand clattered to the floor. "Not grant your wish? That's the most absurd thing I've ever heard in my whole entire fairy life." Fairy Princess Gardengrow huffed. She collected her wand, stood up, and brushed off her flowering dress.

"It's not that I *don't* want it. I absolutely *do*. I would *love* to have my wish come true," Elle said, watching the fairy correct the crown of flowers on her head. "But if you grant my wish, you'll be putting the unicorns in danger. It may even harm all of Avonlea."

"What makes you think that, smart unicorn?" Fairy Princess Gardengrow stood on tiptoe and kissed the unicorn on her nose.

"I cannot leave my post in the Kingdom of Summerstart. I'm the only unicorn in the kingdom that keeps summer green and lush. I help the clovers grow big and colorful. If I leave, our food supply will be endangered."

"Oh dear, that is a rather large predicament."

"And that's a rather large word." Elle stared at the fairy.

"Pre-dic-a-ment." Fairy Princess Gardengrow lifted into the air. "It means a problem...a difficult situation...one that's hard to get out of." She lifted higher into the air with each phrase she said. "Maybe you should have wished for a bowl of sparkle fruit instead."

Elle turned away. She was embarrassed and ashamed. "I know."

Fairy Princess Gardengrow started to giggle.

She giggled and giggled. She laughed so hard she let out a great, big snort. "Don't be ridiculous, smart unicorn! Your wish is a fine one!"

"It is?" Elle raised her head and turned it sideways, giving Fairy Princess Gardengrow a questioning glance. "You think it's a fine thing to put my friends in danger?"

"Heavens to Avonlea! Of course not!" Fairy Princess Gardengrow twirled about. She pranced around the room, tapping her wand against random objects. First the window, then a vase filled with wildflowers brought in from the meadows of the Kingdom of Springsmorn, until finally she tapped Elle's head. "There's always a solution. And goodness, do I have a sublime one!"

"A sub...what?"

"Sublime." Fairy Princess Gardengrow held Elle's face and looked into her eyes before twirling around. "It means supreme, grand, outstanding, elevated, wonderful." With each word, Fairy Princess Gardengrow fluttered higher and higher until she had reached the ceiling.

"Oh, I see." Elle craned her head to look up. "So, you're saying you have a good idea."

"Precisely," Fairy Princess Gardengrow said, fluttering back down until she landed softly, her tiny feet barely making a sound. "Now, hold still. This won't hurt a bit."

"You've said that before. I'm beginning to think it might not be true."

Fairy Princess Gardengrow chuckled. She tapped the unicorn's head with her wand and fairy dust sprinkled out everywhere coating Elle's fur with glitter. Fairy Princess Gardengrow spun in a circle. "Now, to grant your wish."

Elle laughed. "You mean the glitter wasn't part of it?"

"Not at all. I just wanted to add a little birthday sparkle."

Elle's skin began to itch, and she shook the glitter from her fur.

Fairy Princess Gardengrow stood in front of the window again, gazing out into the Kingdom of Summerstart. The sun was beginning to rise, and it cast an orange glow throughout the kingdom. "There is only one way for your wish to come true. You're right, Elle." The fairy's shoulders rose as she took a deep breath. "This wish does come with great risk."

"I knew it would," Elle said feeling horrible about her selfish request.

"But you need not worry about your friends or your kingdom."

Elle's ears perked. "That's wonderful news!"

"No, my smart unicorn friend." The fairy turned around, her face quite serious. "The risk is on you."

Chapter 8

"*M*e?" Elle's legs wobbled beneath her. The room swirled around her and she felt dizzy.

"Steady, steady." Fairy Princess Gardengrow rushed over to Elle's side and helped her regain her balance.

Elle was glad to hear the kingdom would be fine and that her friends wouldn't be harmed. This was a big relief. She could have her wish fulfilled without harm to others. *But,* she wondered, *am I willing to endanger myself?* "What kind of risk?"

"I need to know first if you're willing to do it." Fairy Princess Gardengrow waved her wand and it sputtered. A few sparkles fizzled to the ground. "This old wand. Always having fits." She tapped the twig on the table. A green vine shout out. It was covered in flowers just like her dress. "Oh, that's not what I wanted you to do." She shook the wand and it sprung to life with a stream of glitter. "That's more like it. Now, where were we?"

"I need to know what the danger is." Elle didn't want to agree to something without first knowing the details.

"Oh right." Fairy Princess Gardengrow danced about the room. "Tra-la-la-la-la. You must agree first. If you don't, you'll never get to see a snowstorm and you'll not be able to wish for it ever again."

That doesn't seem fair, Elle thought. But she couldn't take any chances. If what the fairy said was correct, then this was her only hope of ever having her wish come true. Elle stood tall, holding her head high. "I'll do it. I will take the risk so I can see a snowstorm. But you must promise that my friends and the Island of Avonlea will be safe."

"You have my word," Fairy Princess Garden-grow said, patting the unicorn on her head.

"Alright then." Elle nuzzled against the fairy's shoulder. "What do I need to do?"

Fairy Princess Gardengrow began to pace just as she had done before. Her long dress swished and swirled leaving a trail of fairy dust on the floor with every step she took. "The first thing you will need to do is leave the mountain."

"But—" Elle started to speak but was interrupted.

"Shh, shh, shh…" Fairy Princess Gardengrow hushed the unicorn. "Let me finish."

Elle nodded. She swished her tail to and fro as she listened to the fairy's instructions.

"You must go down the mountain and head straight for Will-o'-the-Wisp Woods."

"I have to go in the woods?" Elle gulped. She'd heard scary stories of spooks in those woods. There was no way she wanted to go in there. What if the spooks got her, too?

Fairy Princess Gardengrow crossed her arms and gave Elle a hard stare. "Yes."

"Isn't there an easier way?" Elle stared wide-eyed at the fairy who started to pace again. Elle joined alongside, her golden hooves clip-clop-ping against the floor. "I could go straight through the Kingdom of Summerstart, stay close to the Crystal Palace and then cross over into the Kingdom of Wintersend."

"You might be seen if you go that way. We cannot let the unicorns know you've left your mansion here on the mountain. They might get worried. Then they'll try to stop you. That would mean you won't get your wish." The fairy looked Elle in the eyes. "The only way is to follow the perimeter of the island."

This was another word that Elle didn't understand. "Per—"

"Perimeter," the fairy said, fluttering into the air. "It means the border. The boundary. The outer most edge." Gardengrow lifted higher with each word until she reached the ceiling.

"Oh," Elle swished her tail, deep in thought. "Then what's next?"

Fairy Princess Gardengrow floated back down. "Next you must go through Pixie Place."

Elle gulped. She didn't say a word. Just felt her heart beating as fast as a garden gnome trying to run from a fox. "And then...?"

"Then you'll need to enter Fairy Forest."

Elle had only heard of such a place in her childhood fairy tales. "Will there be other fairies there?"

Fairy Princess Gardengrow nodded. "Yes, there are lots of fairies in the forest."

"Are they good and kind like you?"

"Of course!" Fairy Princess Gardengrow laughed. "Tell them I've sent you."

Elle nodded.

"Now, remember, you must stay near the edge of the island throughout your journey. You cannot go inland at all. The unicorns must not see you."

"Not even one?" Elle felt as though this may be impossible.

The fairy tapped her chin. "You may see Callie once you get to Wintersend. But that is all."

Elle nodded. "Understood."

"You must promise me that you will listen to my request."

"I promise," Elle said. "I will do just as you ask."

Fairy Princess Gardengrow stroked Elle's golden mane. "Good."

"Will you be joining me?" Elle asked as she nuzzled into the fairy.

"No," Fairy Princess Gardengrow said.

"Why not?" Elle asked. Surely Fairy Princess Gardengrow needed to return to Fairy Forest, and this would be a perfect journey to do together. Elle even felt a bit scared to go alone, especially through Will-o'-the-Wisp Woods. There would be safety in numbers.

Fairy Princess Gardengrow stepped away and looked the unicorn in her eyes. "Because I will be caring for your kingdom while you're away."

Impossible! Elle thought. "Only unicorns can do that." Perhaps Elle's travels would be risky but leaving someone else in charge of her kingdom was the biggest risk of all.

Chapter 9

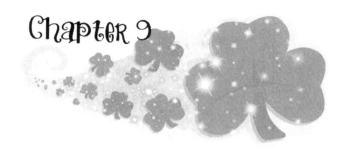

"*D*o you want your wish or not?" Gardengrow asked.

Elle shook her head. This was a very bad idea. Fairy Princess Gardengrow was good and kind but she wasn't a unicorn. Only unicorns were intended to rule over the kingdoms. Leaving a fairy in charge could spell disaster for all of Avonlea.

"Remember, I live on the island, too. I want what's best for it just as much as you do." Gardengrow tapped her wand to her palm as she gazed out the window, looking over the Kingdom of Summerstart.

Elle felt as though she might cry. It was scary leaving someone else in charge. But she felt as though she could trust the fairy because, after all, they lived in the same beautiful world together. "You'll take good care of it?"

"Of course." The fairy nodded with a smile.

The two watched as the clouds thinned and the morning sun made its way into the horizon, casting a golden shade of orange on the kingdom. Night had passed quickly while Elle and Gardengrow discussed the secret wish and plans to make it come true.

In the distance, Anna frolicked in a field. She was headed toward the Colorful Clover Patch. Clovers were harvested daily, and it needed to be done early before the heat of the day wilted the tasty buds. Soon Maureen and Bonnie would join her.

"Don't worry," Fairy Princess Gardengrow said. "I will care for your kingdom as if it were my own. I promise you are leaving it in good hands."

Elle whinnied. "Thank you."

The fairy turned on her heel and patted the unicorn's head. "Now, there's one other thing you must know."

Elle flicked her tail, wondering why there were so many rules to getting this wish. "What is it?" she asked, looking straight into the fairy's eyes.

"You must see the snowstorm before sunset.

And you must return to Summerstart before the next sunrise."

Elle gasped. "But it'll take most of the morning just to get to Pixie Place."

"Then you must be on your way. Take these with you," Fairy Princess Gardengrow said as she filled a bag with sparkle fruit left over from the party. "And these." In another bag she placed hollyberries and clovers. She tied the two bags together and laid them across Elle's back like a saddle.

"And if I don't return in time?" Elle asked, almost afraid to hear the answer.

"Then it's possible the island will be harmed. If you're gone too long, you would deprive Summerstart of your powers. Your magic is strong, smart unicorn. If you're in Wintersend too long, you could hurt it with your powers."

"How terrible," Elle whinnied. "I wouldn't want to do that."

"That's why you must hurry!"

Without a second thought, Elle bolted through the front door of her mansion. She didn't look back but went straight down the mountain, stumbling over rocks and cliffs. As soon as she reached the bottom, she saw

Maureen and Bonnie walking along Rainbow River toward South Lake. The two stopped and took a drink. Elle quickly ducked behind a tree. She had to obey the fairy's command and hide herself. It was the only way to have her birthday wish fulfilled.

As soon as her friends had passed, she trotted off toward Will-o'-the-Wisp Woods. When she reached the forest, she stood at the entrance shaking in fear. Goosebumps rose up on her skin. She shook her mane trying to chase the chill of fear away.

"It'll be fine. Everything will be fine. There is nothing to be afraid of. Spooks aren't real." Elle tipped her head back, putting her nose into the air, and took a deep breath. With a neigh, she reared back, then galloped into the woods.

As soon as she entered, cold air swept across her fur. Even though it was morning, the forest was dark. Almost as dark as night. The trees were so dense and the leaves so full, it blocked out nearly all the sunlight.

Elle wished she had a lantern to light her path. But she was unprepared for her journey, except for the bit of food and treats Fairy Princess Gardengrow had packed for her. She'd just have to push forward through the forest without it. Maybe her eyes would adjust to the darkness.

Carefully trotting through the woods, Elle avoided thorny bushes, and low branches. She tried not to think of the spooks. Those stories couldn't be true. She refused to believe them. But her heart beat faster. Her breath caught in her throat. She was scared.

As Elle dodged and weaved, she became dizzy. The darkness swirled around her and she turned in circles. "Where am I?" she cried, her voice coming out in a fearful neigh. She looked side to side trying to find her way. "I'll never get out of here!"

Elle was upset and scared.

She shouldn't have wished to see a snowstorm.

She shouldn't have left her home.

She shouldn't have gone into the forest.

Now she'd be lost forever, she'd never get her wish, and Avonlea would be in danger. "What did I do?" Elle whinnied as she reared up, kicking her hooves in the air. Tears leaked from her eyes.

Things couldn't have been worse, and Elle

felt terrible. She laid on the mossy earth and cried. After a short while, Elle took a deep breath and blinked away her tears. Out of the corner of her eye, she saw a flicker of light. Elle turned her head sharply.

"Is that what I think it is?" Elle stood up and shook her golden mane. She squinted and the light glowed brighter and brighter. "It is! Just there. A light! That must be the end of the forest," she exclaimed.

Elle galloped toward the light. Branches slapped her face, thicket clawed at her legs, but she didn't mind. She was almost out of the forest and soon she'd arrive in the Kingdom of Springsmorn. It wouldn't be long now, and she'd finally see her wish come true!

Chapter 10

As Elle sprinted toward the light with her heart thudding in excitement, she felt so much joy. Her wish was about to come true! She'd finally get to see a snowstorm!

"C'mon legs," Elle said as she galloped. "We're almost there! Follow the light." She ducked under a low-laying branch, turning her head ever so slightly. When she righted herself, the light was gone.

Elle screeched to a halt. "It disappeared," she choked out between breaths. "How can that be?"

Lowering her head, Elle saw another flickering. This one was close to the ground and it seemed to blink on and off, as it darted off deep into the forest. Elle trotted toward it, changing course as the light did. It would flicker and then appear in another spot. *If only it would stay lit until I reached it,* Elle thought, *then I'd find my way out in no time!* But the closer she got, the dimmer it became until it blinked out completely.

"Impossible! It's gone again!" Elle cried. It was so strange for a light to simply disappear. "The trees are too thick. That must be it. The leaves are blocking the light." Elle trusted her instincts. She felt hopeful the light would appear again. She just had to keep walking.

Thankfully, she was right. A light blinked on. But it didn't come from where she expected. Instead of it being low to the ground, it was at eye level. "There it is!" she neighed. "If I want out of here, I have to follow the light."

Elle cantered toward the warm, glow of gold that promised the fulfillment of her wish. Feeling worried the light would vanish just as the others had, she increased her speed until she was galloping through the woods.

Following the light while dodging branches, leaping over mounds of rocks and moss, and avoiding thorny bushes, Elle ran deeper and deeper into the forest.

She gained on the light, bringing it closer and closer into view. "Almost there!" she panted.

When the light was only inches away, it disappeared!

"No, no, no!" Elle cried between pants. "That's impossible! What's going on in these woods?" She felt spooked, scared, and all alone.

Suddenly, a branched snapped behind her. Elle reared up with a whinny and took off in a bolt, her bags of food flying off her back. She ran even deeper into the forest. Further than she ever thought possible. She'd never been in the Will-o'-the-Wisp Woods before and she had no idea they were so large. It would be easy for a unicorn to get lost. In fact, she was sure that's just what had happened to her.

"Oh no!" Elle cried. "I'm lost!" She had no idea of which way was forward, which way was backward, or anything in between. She'd never find her way through the forest and she'd never have her wish fulfilled. Worse, she'd never return to her mansion on top of Mount Summerstart. Without Elle's guidance, she was sure the kingdom could fall apart. "This is a disaster."

Elle hung her head, wondering why she'd made the wish in the first place. Why, oh, why had she agreed to Fairy Princess Gardengrow's requests? This all had been a big mistake. Elle brushed up against a tree, the scratchy bark rubbing against her golden coat. Leaves rustled behind her and Elle quickly whirled around. "Who's there?"

A little giggle fluttered on a breeze.

"Who's laughing?" Elle called into the dark, empty woods. She trembled, feeling terribly afraid. "It's just my imagination. I'm hearing things because I'm scared. There's no one here but me and the trees."

"Are you sure about that?" a little voice asked.

Elle gasped and stumbled back. "Who's there?"

"Careful!" the voice said. "You're stepping on my beard!"

"And you've put a hole in the roof of my house!" another voice said.

Elle glanced down and saw something she never thought possible.

Chapter 11

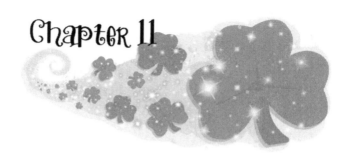

Hundreds of gnomes dotted the forest floor. "Garden gnomes?" Elle blinked as she stared at the chubby little creatures, all with big noses and small eyes who stood no taller than the stump of a tree. Some had long beards and wore pointed hats made of moss. Others had blushed cheeks, flower crowns, and dresses made of leaves.

"Forest gnomes to be exact," a girl with particularly long brown hair said. She tripped on her locks as she took a step forward. "My name is Fern."

"I...I..." Elle stuttered.

"What?" Another gnome wearing trousers with wide suspenders folded his arms with a humpf.

"I didn't know forest gnomes existed. I just thought—"

"We were make-believe?" The gnome wearing suspenders groaned. "We're gnomes."

"Oh, well of course you are." Elle hadn't meant to be rude. She pawed at the ground with her hoof.

"Excuse me," the gnome at her hoof said. "Would you mind stepping back? You're pulling on my beard."

"My apologies." Elle blushed. She lifted her hoof and the gnome quickly collected his beard, tucking it under his arm.

"The name's Leif," he said.

"Nice to meet you. My name is Elle."

Fern's eyes grew large as she gasped. "The unicorn of Summerstart? The one who makes sure the clovers grow?"

Elle nodded.

"Goodness gracious to Avonlea!" Fern grabbed Leif's hand and the two bowed at Elle's hooves.

"Mind if I ask what you're doing in our forest?" Leif asked.

"It's a long story," Elle said. "I'm not sure where to start."

"Try the beginning," Fern, the brown-haired gnome, said. "Now tell us your tale."

"Not the beginning," Leif said looking at Fern with a raised brow. "That's boring. Start at the moment you met us. Now that's interesting," he said to Elle.

"Don't be silly, Leif," Fern said. "There's nothing to tell."

"Of course, there is!" Leif crossed his arms and began to pace. "This unicorn trampled our houses, nearly ripped my beard off, and thought we were make-believe! There's plenty of story right there. Root," he said, turning to a gnome seated on a pile of rocks. "Write that down!"

Root used a feather pen to take notes on a piece of bark, never once looking up.

"Don't mind him," Fern said. "He makes a mountain out of a mole hill for everything."

"Thanks to this clumsy unicorn—"

"Elle the unicorn," Fern corrected.

"Right. Well, all I have is a pile of rocks." Leif grunted and sat at the base of a tree.

"I'm sorry about that," Elle said. "I had no idea they were your homes."

"Well, now you do!" Leif twirled his white mustache.

"It was so dark, I couldn't see very well," Elle said as she flicked her tail. "And I was trying to follow the light, but it seemed to move every time I got close."

"Will-o-the-Wisps!" Fern shouted. "Those little trouble-makers will get you every time!" She turned to Leif. "See, I told you we needed the story from the beginning!"

"Bah!" Leif folded his arms and turned his back.

"Go on, dear," Fern said to Elle. "We'd like to hear more of this story."

"I'm afraid I don't have time. But if you could tell me how to get out of the forest, I'd be ever so grateful."

"Which direction, dear?" Fern asked.

Elle bowed her head and whispered, "The Kingdom of Springsmorn."

"You're going to another kingdom?" Fern asked with a gasp.

"It's a birthday wish. I'll be quick. I promise."

Fern nodded. "Follow that path." She pointed to a pile of rocks that seemed to create a curved trail. "It'll take you right there."

"Thank you, Fern." Elle shook her mane. "I shall award you a special title. Fern the Fantastic."

Fern blushed. "Now, be careful of those

Wisps. Whatever you do, you must ignore them!"

"I can do that," Elle said. "Thank you for your help." Elle followed the trail of rocks. As she did, she saw more gnomes. Those rocks weren't just a path. They were gnome homes!

As Elle carefully stepped along, trying to avoid trampling the houses, a light flickered. "I'll get those Will-o-the-Wisps!" she whispered. Elle blinked and quietly crept toward the light. She stepped over broken branches. She avoided piles of leaves. Patches of moss softened the sound of her hooves on the earth.

Another light flickered on. This one on her left. Elle stepped sideways.

Then one flickered at her right. "Will-O'-The-Wisps!" She backed away.

A light flickered in the sky. Elle twirled. "You pests!"

Then another at her feet. "Go away, spooks!" She zig-zagged.

Then another, and another, and another until there were so many lights Elle was running in circles. Elle was so dizzy the lights became a blur. She didn't know which direction she'd come from or which way to go. Elle was lost again!

Chapter 12

"I'm lost!" Elle cried. "And it's all your fault." She flicked her tail toward the will-o'-the-wisps.

"We're sorry," a will-o'-the-wisp said. "We didn't mean to cause trouble."

Another wisp giggled. "Our lights have a mind of their own."

"We can help you," the first wisp said.

"You can?" Elle didn't believe them. The gnome named Fern had told her to ignore the wisps. Elle hadn't listened and now she was lost. Elle felt maybe she was making another mistake by talking to them. Maybe they'd lead her astray.

"Just follow your nose," the wisp said with a giggle.

That's silly, Elle thought. *My nose is on my face. I can't follow it.*

Another wisp blinked on, glowing a soft shade of yellow. "If you smell something nice it might lead you where you long to go."

There was nothing better than the sweet fragrance of sparkle fruit. And sparkle fruit was in the Kingdom of Springsmorn. If she followed the smell, she'd find her way. The wisps were right!

"Brilliant!" Elle said as she lifted her head, sniffing the air. The sweetness of sparkle fruit was off to her right. She turned her head left and smelled the colorful clovers far off in Summerstart. Elle perked her ears and listened. The sound of water rushed straight ahead. "Rainbow River," she whispered. "I know which way to go!"

"Good luck, unicorn," a wisp giggled.

Elle galloped as fast as she could through the thicket of brush and the cover of trees. Branches slapped against her hind quarters and the briars scratched her face. She pushed through despite the sting. She didn't have any more time to waste. Elle had been lost in the Will-o'-the-Wisp Woods for far too long. She'd have to hurry through the rest of her journey if she wanted to see the snowstorm and return to her kingdom on time.

Out of breath and panting, Elle finally reached the edge of the woods. She burst out from the trees onto dewy grass. Daylight colored the ground a brilliant shade of lime. "I did it," she panted. "I made it through the Will-o'-the-Wisp Woods!" She danced in a circle, twisting about, and throwing her head back. Her golden mane glistened in the sunshine.

As Elle celebrated, she trotted along Rainbow River and then turned right into the

Kingdom of Springsmorn. She pranced straight into the Sparkle Fruit Garden. Elle's stomach grumbled as the fragrance of the yummy fruit tickled her nose. "It's lunchtime and I can't continue without food," she said eyeing the delicious fruit. "I could eat it quickly and then be on my way."

As she reached for a piece, ready to pluck it from a tree, two unicorns trotted toward the garden. It was Maeve and Fiona! Elle smiled and neighed. What a relief it was to see friendly faces! Elle neighed again, pawing her hooves at the ground. The two unicorns startled.

Maeve glanced at Fiona. "Did you hear that?"

"It's me," Elle said. But she suddenly remembered Gardengrow's instructions. Stay hidden or the unicorns may worry. In her excitement, Elle had nearly forgotten the rules. She quickly ducked between trees.

"Must be the spooks in the forest of Summerstart," Fiona said.

"Or the trouble-making pixies," Maeve said. "Hurry, let's go to the meadow before either of them find us."

Elle watched as her two friends went on

their way. "Phew," she said with a sigh of relief. "I'm so glad they didn't see me."

As soon as Maeve and Fiona were out of sight, Elle continued on her journey toward the Kingdom of Wintersend. If she followed the perimeter, as Fairy Princess Gardengrow advised, the path would lead her through Pixie Place next. Thankfully, it didn't sound quite as scary as Will-o'-the-Wisp Woods.

"I've made it to Pixie Place!" Elle said as she approached a large tree.

"Star Hollow," a voice said. It seemed to come from the tree. But that was impossible.

"It's splendid! I've never seen anything quite like it," Elle said.

Suddenly, a chorus of voices rang out. Elle twirled around and saw three pixies. They were making a ruckus, zipping and zooming, dodging flowers and birds. Pixie dust trailed from their feet. They darted toward Elle.

"Let's get her!" a pixie said as she pointed at the unicorn.

Chapter 13

*E*lle whinnied with fear. *Oh no! They see me! Now I'll never get to see my wish come true.*

The three pixies flew straight at Elle. She ducked out of the way just as a little dark-haired pixie darted toward her, skimming Elle's ear. The pixies didn't stop. They kept on flying, looping into the branches of the great tree. "Whoa," Elle cried. "That was a close one."

A fourth pixie wearing a pink dress tucked behind a flowering branch of the tree. The three pixies teamed together and chased her.

"That poor little pixie. She needs my help." Elle was about to offer assistance but as soon as she took a step, the branch of the tree slapped her hind quarters.

"Move along!" the tree said.

"Oh, oh, oh!" Elle reared up with a loud neigh.

"Go on!" The tree flicked it's branch at Elle again.

"My goodness!" Elle cried. She didn't know that trees could talk. She also didn't know they could be so mean. She always imagined if trees could say anything, they would be kind and not quite so abrasive. "Yes, of course."

"I'm sorry to scare you," the tree said. "My name is Willow. And you are in Star Hollow. Pixie Place is that way." The tree shook its branches and the four pixies scattered, flying in the direction that the tree pointed.

Elle stood staring at the tree in awe. "It's a beautiful place."

"It's growing late," Willow said with a yawn. "You must get going or you won't make it in time."

Elle backed away. "Not only can you talk but you seem to know…"

"I see everything. I hear everything. I know all." The tree's branches dipped low to the ground, making a soft breeze as it bowed. "Now, hurry. You don't want to miss the snowstorm. I understand this is a very special birthday wish."

Elle nodded. "You're a wise one. Remind me to award you a special title once I return to Summerstart."

Willow, the Star Hollow tree, curled it's branches into its trunk and bowed. "It would be my honor. Now hurry. You must go!"

Elle chuffed and cantered into Pixie Place. Dozens of pixies buzzed about. Glitter rained down as they busied themselves darting from one branch to another. All of them seemed to be watching Elle. They whispered and giggled but never approached. In fact, if Elle got too close, they darted off into the treetops. "I won't hurt you," she whispered. But the pixies kept their distance. Soon, Elle had reached the other side, leaving the magic of Pixie Place behind her.

When Elle approached the valley between the two kingdoms, she shivered as a chill from the cool air of Wintersend fell upon her fur like a blanket of ice. She had felt this before when Callie was near.

Elle glanced at the mountains to her right. The base was densely populated with trees.

"That must be Fairy Forest." Elle squinted, trying to see between the branches. Would she have to face scary things inside the forest?

Chapter 14

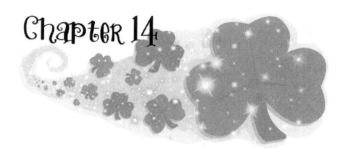

*E*lle stepped inside Fairy Forest with a shiver and it seemed to welcome her. Trees hugged her as she brushed past. They were different than anything she'd ever seen before. Instead of wide leaves covering the tips of the branches, there were little needles of various shades of purples, blues, greens, and yellows. The thin needles allowed more sun to filter through and yet it kept the cold out, too. But Elle questioned if she'd be able to see a snowstorm through the treetops.

As Elle walked amongst the trees, she noticed they were decorated. Each tree had clusters of silver bells, clovers, hollyberries, sparkle fruit, and ornaments in the shape of unicorns. One tree was entirely decorated in yellow. Elle gasped when she saw an ornament that looked just like her. "Hello? Is anyone here? It's me. Elle the unicorn, from the Kingdom of Summerstart." But there was no response. There was no one to be seen in the forest. Not a single fairy. "This is the oddest place ever."

"We think it's magical," a voice said from behind her.

Elle twirled around, her horn smacking into the limb of a tree. Two ornaments toppled off the branch and shattered to the ground. "I'm sorry. I didn't mean to break them."

Glitter swirled around the ornaments, lifting them into the air. In an instant, they were repaired and placed back onto the tree. "No harm done," the voice said.

Elle searched around her but saw no one. "Where are you?"

"Right here!" the voice said. A fairy twirled out from behind a tree, her long dress trickling like a babbling brook. "I'm Fairy Princess Waterfall." The fairy princess's beautiful gown shimmered with shades of blue and white. Little pearls in the shape of raindrops trimmed her dress. Her sleeves were poofed up, just like clouds. She had pointed wings speckled with raindrops. The fairy princess had a round face, tiny lips, and hair the color of the sky. "And this is my friend, Fairy Princess Rainbow."

The other fairy bowed. Her crown slipped, and she gently pushed it back in place. When she stood, Elle gasped in awe of the fairy's dress. It cascaded from her waist to the ground in a prism of colors.

"Hello, Elle," Fairy Princess Rainbow said. "We've been waiting for you."

"You have?" Elle stared at them both wide-eyed. She stomped her front hoof on the ground in excitement.

"Fairy Princess Gardengrow told us you'd be coming to have your birthday wish fulfilled."

Elle nodded. "Why yes, that's precisely why I'm here."

"Well, then we're ready to help." Fairy Princess Rainbow stroked Elle's golden mane.

"You're going to help me?" Elle looked from one fairy to the other, her tail swishing with each turn of her head.

Fairy Princess Waterfall nodded. "We'll take you up the mountain to see the king."

"The king?" Elle didn't know she'd have to meet someone so important.

"Yes, King Hollyberry," Fairy Princess

Rainbow said. "He will help you with the rest of your request."

"The mountain is dangerous, Rainbow," Fairy Princess Waterfall said. "We can't send her that way."

Elle felt relieved. She didn't want to face any danger. Still, she knew time was running out. If this was the only way to have her wish fulfilled, she needed to do it fast.

"But it's the only way to get to the king," Fairy Princess Rainbow said.

Sadly, Elle realized this meant her wish was at stake. "If we don't go up the mountain, then how am I to see a snowstorm?"

"We could bring the king to her," Fairy Princess Waterfall said.

"No, that would take too long. I need to see the snowstorm before sunset." Elle looked at the faces of the two fairies. "And I must return to my kingdom before sunrise."

"Then there must be another way," Fairy Princess Rainbow said.

Elle had an idea that might just solve the problem.

Chapter 15

"*D*oesn't Callie control the snow?" Elle asked. "Couldn't she show me?"

"Why, of course!" Fairy Princess Rainbow twirled around, her colorful dress fanning out around her. "Why didn't I think of that?"

"I should have been the one to think of it." Fairy Princess Waterfall slumped down on a large rock shaped like a toadstool.

"It doesn't matter who came up with the idea," Elle said, nudging Fairy Princess Waterfall with her nose. "All that matters is that someone can take me to see her."

"Couldn't Callie have just come to you?" Fairy Princess Rainbow asked. "That would have been much easier than having you travel all this way."

"It's much too warm in Summerstart. The

snow would melt instantly." Elle pawed at the ground. "The only choice was to come here."

"Fairy Princess Gardengrow sure is smart!" Waterfall said.

Rainbow giggled. "Indeed."

"Can you take me to see Callie?" Elle asked. She needed to get the fairies back on track before time ran out.

"That's the easy part!" Fairy Princess Waterfall twirled. She spun so fast her feet lifted off the ground. Her beautiful wings fluttered, lifting her higher into the air until she flittered above Elle's head.

Elle watched in amazement. "Wonderful! I'm ready."

"Then we shall go!" A tear rolled down Waterfall's cheek.

"Why are you sad?" Elle asked.

"I'm not sad," Fairy Princess Waterfall said. "I'm leaking."

"Oh, don't mind her," Rainbow said. "She always does that."

"Leaking?" Elle stared at the fairy, feeling quite puzzled.

"It happens when I'm overdue for a rain shower." Fairy Princess Waterfall leaked more tears as she spoke. "I've been waiting on Maeve, but she hasn't called on me in a while."

"You're Maeve's fairy?" Elle gasped.

"I certainly am!" Waterfall said with a giggle. "Every unicorn has a special fairy."

"Then that's why Fairy Princess Gardengrow came to me. She's the only one who can fulfill my wishes." Elle finally understood why everything had happened.

"That's right," Fairy Princess Rainbow said. "Now, let's see if we can help you with your wish. We will take you to Callie and she will grant you a snowstorm."

"Maybe we should invite Fairy Princess Snowflurry along?" Waterfall said.

"Good idea!" Rainbow smiled. "Why don't you get her?"

Waterfall nodded before darting off. A few moments later she returned with Fairy Princess Snowflurry.

"I've come to join you!" Snowflurry said with a twirl of her sparkling dress.

"Wonderful!" Elle neighed. "Let's hurry before the sun sets!"

The three fairies led Elle out of Fairy Forest

into the open space of the Kingdom of Wintersend.

White dust blanketed the ground. "What is this?" Elle kicked her hoof into the powder. It blew into the air and showered back down to the ground.

"It's snow!" Fairy Princess Rainbow said.

"This is snow?" Elle dropped to the ground and began rolling around. She rubbed her back into the cold powder. She rolled from side to side. She neighed and whinnied with delight. "It's cold and wet and oh so fun!"

"Come now." Fairy Princess Rainbow gave a gentle tug on Elle's mane. "We've no time for games."

Elle leapt up and shook the snow from her fur. It flew out like glitter. Most of it fluttered to the ground but some of it floated off into the breeze. She watched it with delight. "I'm coming."

The four friends walked toward the town. There were pegacorns prancing about everywhere. Some in the market square, others going in and out of shops. A few walking up and down the street. Elle suddenly dug her hooves into the ground, refusing to take another step.

"What's wrong?" Fairy Princess Waterfall asked.

"Oh no! I can't let them see me." Elle ducked behind a cottage. Puffs of smoke lifted from the chimney into the air.

"Why not?" Rainbow asked.

"Fairy Princess Gardengrow told me to be careful. She gave me special instructions to follow. The other unicorns must never know that I've left my post in Summerstart." Elle shook her head realizing her mistake. "If the pegacorns in Wintersend see me, they'll know I'm not where I should be. They'll send me home and then I'll never get my wish."

Chapter 16

"Maybe we should have Elle stay behind and we can get Callie for her?" Fairy Princess Waterfall flittered into the air, bouncing about like a kite on the breeze.

"We really shouldn't," Rainbow said. "Elle won't be protected if she's alone."

"But I could go," Snowflurry said. "The three of you could stay here."

"No, no. Fairy Princess Rainbow is right. I need to be able to do this for myself. But I'm worried about Avonlea. I can't put it at risk."

Fairy Princess Rainbow stroked Elle's mane. "Didn't you say that Gardengrow had come to grant your wish?"

"I did," Elle said with a nod. "She promised to stay in my mansion and watch over my kingdom."

"Then she'll protect it." Rainbow patted

Elle's shoulder. "Don't worry, sweet unicorn. Gardengrow is good for her promises."

Elle pawed at the ground. "But what if I'm seen? I can't take that risk. I won't break my promise to Gardengrow. My wish is impossible!"

"We'll make sure you stay hidden." Rainbow danced around Elle. "Now, let's bring you to Callie so you can have your wish!"

"Are you sure it's safe?" Elle's breath fogged up a window on the cottage as she spoke. The air was cold, and the sun was setting in the distance. If she didn't see the snowstorm soon, she never would.

"I'm positive," Fairy Princess Rainbow said.

"And what about her?" Elle looked up at Fairy Princess Waterfall who was still bouncing about like a balloon. Water droplets leaked from the fairy's eyes. They froze into ice as they dripped to the ground, landing with a tinkling sound.

"She'll join us." Fairy Princess Rainbow tugged on the hem of Waterfall's dress. "Come down now."

"But it's so fun," Fairy Princess Waterfall said with a giggle as she bounced on the breeze. More of the fairy's tears dripped from her face and turned into ice. "I didn't know I could make hail."

"You can't," Fairy Princess Snowflurry said. "It's the freezing temperature that's turning your water into ice. You can thank Maribel and Fairy Princess Windstorm for lowering the temperatures with their breezes."

Rainbow pulled on Waterfall's dress again. "Can we get to work?"

Fairy Princess Waterfall folded her arms in a huff. The tears stopped and so did her laughter as she floated back down to the ground. "Fine. But you're not any fun."

"We're in a hurry. Time to focus. Elle needs our help." Fairy Princess Rainbow joined hands with the other two fairies. "Now, let's go."

Elle and the three fairies tiptoed along the edge of town. When a pegacorn cantered past, the fairies stood in front of Elle, shielding her from view.

"Hurry," Fairy Princess Rainbow muttered under her breath. "We've no time to waste."

"Where are you Callie?" Snowflurry called out as she glanced around.

"I'm right here!" Callie circled overhead before landing in front of the fairies. "Did you need me?"

"Not us," the fairies sang in unison. "But she does." They stepped aside revealing Elle who stood behind them.

"Whoa!" Callie gasped. "What are you doing here, Elle?"

Elle bowed her head, embarrassed that she'd come all this way for such a silly wish. Afterall, who wishes to see a snowstorm for their birthday? Most unicorns wish for presents and gifts. None would ever wish for something related to the weather. It was unheard of.

"Elle?" Callie neighed softly. "Is everything alright? Is Summerstart in danger?"

"The kingdom is fine. Fairy Princess Gardengrow is watching over it," Waterfall said as she twittered about. "But no one can know Elle's here. It's a secret."

"I can keep a secret." Callie winked at Elle. "Now, how can I help?"

Elle neighed and shook her head.

Fairy Princess Rainbow stroked Elle's mane of long, flowing golden hair. "It's alright, sweet unicorn. Tell your friend your wish."

Callie pounded her hooves on the ground in excitement. "What kind of wish?"

"It's for my birthday," Elle said without looking up. "Morgan had placed a magic candle on my cake."

Callie stopped suddenly. "Are you sure?"

"Positive." Elle nodded, still looking at the ground.

"What did you wish for?" Callie beat her wings twice as she waited for Elle's answer.

Elle felt ashamed to admit it to her friend. "I wished to see a snowstorm."

Callie gasped and stumbled backward.

This was turning out terrible and Elle felt horrible for such a silly and dangerous birthday wish.

Chapter 17

*E*lle finally looked up fearing the disappointment in her friend's face. "I'm sorry. I know it was wrong. I shouldn't have—"

"You've come to the right place!" Callie exclaimed with delight. "We love snowstorms in the Kingdom of Wintersend and I'm just the pegacorn for the job. I'm delighted to grant your wish!"

"You're not angry?" Elle blinked. "You don't think I'm foolish?"

"Foolish?" Callie coughed. "Heavens no," she said with a laugh. "It was just brilliant for you to come here. If I'd brought snow to the Kingdom of Summerstart it would have ruined the island."

"Or it would have melted before it reached the ground," Fairy Princess Snowflurry said.

"That's true." Callie rubbed her head against Snowflurry who stroked her mane. "And that would have been pointless."

"Exactly." Snowflurry nodded.

"It wasn't entirely my idea." Elle thought back to the beautiful fairy who arrived at her house after all the guests had left. "I had some help from Fairy Princess Gardengrow. And Morgan's magic candle."

"Of course, you did." Callie laughed again. This time she nearly fell over she laughed so hard.

"What's so funny?" Elle asked as she watched her friend.

Callie circled around Elle. "You made a wish, didn't you?"

"Of course, I did." Elle turned about as Callie stopped in front of her.

"You didn't need a magic candle for that," Callie said. "Your fairy came because she heard your wish. She would have come had you wished on a shooting star or your bowl of colorful clovers." Callie winked at Fairy Princess Snowflurry who nodded with a knowing smile.

"Ohhhh," Elle said.

"Now, did someone wish for a snowstorm?" Callie reared up on her hind legs and beat her wings. The air moved so fast and hard Elle had to turn her head away from the breeze.

"I did!" Elle laughed. "I wished for a snowstorm!"

"Then," Callie said as she flew into the sky, "a snowstorm is just what you shall get!"

Callie soared above the mountains, way up into the clouds. She was so high, Elle almost couldn't see her anymore and she squinted as she stared into the heavens.

"Will the snow start soon?" Elle asked, gazing up into the clouds.

"Any moment," Fairy Princess Snowflurry said. "Patience my dear unicorn. Patience."

As if on command, flakes of white started falling from the sky. Big ones, little ones. They danced about in the breeze.

"Whoa," Elle said, watching as the snow flurried down. She couldn't believe her eyes. She knew all the unicorns had magic. Even she had her very own gift of helping the plants grow in the Kingdom of Summerstart. Without Elle, the colorful clovers would surely wilt away, and the unicorns would go hungry. Elle turned toward Fairy Princess Snowflurry. "She really did that?"

"Yes. She sure did!" Snowflurry tipped her head back, closed her eyes, and twirled about in the fluttering snowflakes.

"It's beautiful, Callie," Elle shouted toward the heavens. "I never knew a snowstorm could be such a wonderful gift." She stuck out her tongue, letting a flake land on it. Within seconds it melted away. "A magical gift."

The snow came down heavier now. Large flakes fell from the sky. Each one had a unique shape. Some like stars, some like flowers. Each of them like nothing Elle had ever seen before.

In minutes, the snow began to gather around Elle's ankles. "I think that's enough," she shouted up to Callie who was still zooming through the sky sending a shower of snow down on everything below.

"Just a bit more," Callie said. "There needs to be enough for—"

"For what?" Elle asked before Callie could finish.

"For this," Fairy Princess Snowflurry twirled her wand in the air. A large clear board appeared.

Elle had never seen anything like it. "What's that?"

"It's a sled," Snowflurry said as she placed it on the ground.

Elle looked at the strange board and wondered how that would help the snow. "What do you do with it?"

"You slide!" Snowflurry said.

"Sledding is one of the best parts of a snowstorm." Callie swooped down and landed near the trio of fairies. "Get on. I'll show you. Ready?"

Elle quickly climbed on. "I think so."

"Let's go!" Callie dug her hoof into the snow, pushed, and the two took off down a small hill.

"Whoa," Elle cried as she steadied herself. Trees whizzed past and Elle closed her eyes. "This is so much fun!"

"I told you!" Callie laughed as the sled slowed to a stop. "Want to go again?"

The sun began to sink in the horizon. It was almost dark. Soon there would be no daylight left. If Elle didn't hurry, she wouldn't make the long journey back to Summerstart before sunrise.

Chapter 18

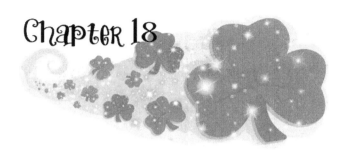

"*I* must go home." Elle was thrilled that she was able to see a snowstorm, but she knew she had to hurry back to Summerstart before she put the kingdoms at risk.

"Don't you worry about that," Callie said with a laugh. "Hop on, you have plenty of time."

"I don't think it's a good idea." Elle shook her head.

"Trust me, friend." Callie neighed and beat her wings.

Elle turned her head and looked at her friend. She knew Callie was trustworthy, but she also knew her journey back would take hours. "If you promise it'll be okay."

Callie nodded. "I promise."

Elle climbed onto the back of the sled and

the two friends slid down the hill, laughing the whole way.

When they returned, Callie rolled around on the ground. "You must make a snow fairy."

"What's that?" Elle asked.

Callie leapt to her feet, revealing a beautiful impression she'd left in the snow.

"Wow!" Elle found a patch of snow and began rolling around. She climbed to her feet and admired her work.

"Not bad for your first try." Callie brushed Elle's shoulder.

"Thank you," Elle said, rubbing her muzzle to Callie's. "You made my birthday wish come true and it was better than I could have ever imagined."

"You're most welcome." Callie flew into the sky. "Now, one last little sprinkling of snow before you leave."

Elle danced about in the shower of flakes, bucking and kicking her hooves in the air.

Callie came in for a landing. "Now, I think you'll need something to remember this forever, don't you?"

"Oh, I will never forget it." Elle was so happy

she felt like this memory would stay with her always.

"Well, I believe an extra special birthday surprise is in order." Callie turned to Fairy Princess Snowflurry. "Do you think you can do it?"

Fairy Princess Snowflurry smiled with a nod. She swirled her wand in the air. Then she twirled around. The snow from the ground spun into a little funnel. Then it grew and grew. Soon it began to take shape. A tiara fit for a princess appeared.

The sparkling crown was shaped like snowflakes. "For me?" Elle bowed before Fairy Princess Snowflurry who placed the crown on the unicorn's head.

"For you," Callie and Snowflurry said in unison.

"When you wear it, may you remember your special wish and just how very brave you are." Snowflurry curtsied at Elle.

"Bravo!" Fairy Princess Rainbow cheered.

Waterfall giggled with joy until tears came from her eyes. "Elle the Brave!"

Elle didn't feel brave but maybe she had been. She had to face her fears in order to receive her wish. All of that required a great deal of risk. She'd traveled through Will-o'-the-Wisp Woods, seen forest gnomes, and nearly been fooled by spooks. She'd found her way through Pixie Place and met the wonderful and mighty Willow. And she'd traveled into the unknown Fairy Forest where she met three new friends. "I guess I am brave," Elle said feeling proud of what she'd done.

"Yes, you are." Callie nudged her friend. "Now, let's get you home."

Snowflurry fashioned the sled into a sleigh by tying it onto Callie's back. "Climb on," she said, pointing her wand toward it. "Callie will fly you home."

Elle's eyes grew wide with excitement. She didn't have to make the long journey back to Summerstart alone. And she would get to fly with Callie!

Before Elle got onto the sled, she turned to the three fairies. "Thank you all so much for your help. I couldn't have done this without you."

"You are most welcome," Fairy Princess Rainbow said.

Waterfall giggled. "Glad to do it."

"Let's go!" Callie lifted into the air, pulling Elle on the sleigh behind her. The two flew off toward Summerstart.

"Wahoo!" Elle neighed. "This is so much fun!" She realized just how lucky Callie was to be able to fly. What a special gift she had. But Elle was special in her own way, too.

Soon they landed on top of Mount Summerstart, right at the door of Elle's mansion.

"I'm home! Thanks to you, friend." Elle now felt an extra special friendship with Callie. "Thank you for the snowstorm and making my birthday wish come true."

"You're welcome. I'm glad I could help." Callie lifted up into the sky. "And don't worry. Your secret is safe with me!" She then flew off toward her home in the Kingdom of Wintersend.

Elle trotted through the door of her mansion, happy and content to be home. Fairy Princess Gardengrow stood by the large picture window, watching over the kingdom just as she had promised. Elle approached her special fairy who helped grant her birthday wish. "And thank you, my dear Fairy Princess Gardengrow, for making it all possible."

"You're welcome, my smart unicorn." Gardengrow rubbed her nose to Elle's. "But the magic was in *you* the whole time."

When her magic fails and her true colors begin to fade, Nadia must find the courage to ask the dragons of Avonlea for help.

AMIE BORST
illustrated by Roch Hercka

I know you've waited a long time for this book and I want to thank you for your patience. Shortly after I wrote this book, my sweet dog crossed the rainbow bridge. I was very sad for a while and didn't feel as though I'd ever be able to look at the story again. Thankfully with time, my heart began to heal and I found the courage to visit this story once more.

As with many of the stories in the Unicorn Tales series, this book is about friendship. It's also about finding courage to do hard things. This seems so appropriate after feeling sad for the loss of my fur baby. So for that reason, this book is for Lily. She was a faithful companion for fourteen years and will always be missed. If you have a pet, I hope you'll treat them with the same love they give you every day. Pets can be our best friends. But pets are also family. Cherish every moment you have together.

I'm grateful we're on this journey together. Thank you for returning to read another book! It warms my heart to know readers enjoy my stories. If you liked this book, please leave a kind review. Reviews will help me reach more readers. Together we can share Unicorn Tales and their message of kindness everywhere!

Thank you for your support!

— AMIE BORST

ABOUT THE AUTHOR

Amie Borst believes in unicorns, loves glitter, and keeps a stash of chocolate hidden away from her chocolate-stealing family. She is the author of several books for children including the Scarily Ever Laughter series (Cinderskella, Little Dead Riding Hood, Snow Fright), the Unicorn Tales series, and the Doomy Prepper series. She's a founding member of From the Mixed-Up Files of Middle-Grade Authors where she contributed for nearly a decade. Please visit her website for more information about school visits and speaking engagements. While you're there, be sure to sign up for her newsletter so you can receive updates on new books, sales, and promotions.

Website: www.amieborst.com

facebook.com/amieborstauthor
instagram.com/amieborst

ABOUT THE ILLUSTRATOR

Roch Hercka is an artist, illustrator, painter, and book lover. This is his second children's book series, having previously illustrated the Scarily Ever Laughter series. Roch enjoys painting, reading comic books, playing board games, and watching movies. He lives in Torun, Poland with his family and a cat. Visit his websites to see more of his beautiful creations!

Illustrations: www.hercka.carbonmade.com
Paintings: www.roch.carbonmade.com

facebook.com/RochHerckaArt
instagram.com/Rochart_85

Made in the USA
Columbia, SC
22 March 2021